The Runaway Egg

For my big sister, Lianne,
and older siblings everywhere . . .
thank you for your patience!

Copyright © 2017 by Katy Hudson

All rights reserved. Published in the United States by
Random House Children's Books,
a division of Penguin Random House LLC, New York.

Random House and the colophon are registered
trademarks of Penguin Random House LLC.

Visit us on the Web! randomhousekids.com

Educators and librarians, for a variety of teaching tools,
visit us at RHTeachersLibrarians.com

Library of Congress Cataloging-in-Publication Data is
available upon request.
    ISBN 978-0-553-52319-5 (trade)
    ISBN 978-0-553-52320-1 (lib. bdg.)
    ISBN 978-0-553-52321-8 (ebook)

MANUFACTURED IN CHINA
10 9 8 7 6 5 4 3 2 1
First Edition

The Runaway Egg

by
Katy Hudson

Random House 🏠 New York

Mama Hen said, "Chick, would you watch your baby brother for a bit? Keep him safe and warm until I get back."

"But why do I need to watch him? All he does is sit. It's not like he's *going* anywhere."

Chick looked at his little brother and could not see what all the fuss was about.

He decided his new brother was very dull.

"I can watch him with my eyes closed," he thought.

Soon Chick fell asleep.

As Chick lay snoozing, there was a

"CRACK"…

then another

"CRACK"…

and off he ran!

Chick raced after his little brother
and was just in time to see him disappear.

"Oh no!" cried Chick.

"Wait!" he called. "Stop, little brother!"

Baa

But his little brother just bounced out of the pigsty and kept going.

NO ENTRY

Chick caught up with his
little brother just in time to see . . .

GULP.
Chick tiptoed around the bull.
Closer . . . closer . . .
But then . . .

What should he do?!
Chick took a deep breath and . . .

The bull didn't
like that one bit.

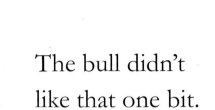

Achooo!

Chick grabbed his little brother and . . .

RAN back home . . .

. . . just in time to see Mama Hen return.

"Look, Chick!" said Mama Hen.
"Your baby brother is hatching!

"Are you ready to be a big brother?"

"As ready as I'll ever be!"